THE VERY CRANKY BEAR

To Tom and Sam. NB.

Scholastic Press
345 Pacific Highway
Lindfield NSW 2070
An imprint of Scholastic Australia Pty Limited
(ABN 11 000 614 577)
PO Box 579
Gosford NSW 2250
www.scholastic.com.au

Part of the Scholastic Group
Sydney • Auckland • New York • Toronto • London • Mexico City
• New Delhi • Hong Kong • Buenos Aires • Puerto Rico

First published by Scholastic Australia in 2008.
Text and illustrations copyright © Nicholas Bland, 2008.

ISBN-10: 0-545-21355-X
ISBN-13: 978-0-545-21355-4

National Library of Australia Cataloguing-in-Publication entry
Bland, Nick.
    The very cranky bear.
    For pre-school age.
    ISBN 9781741691344 (hbk.).
    I. Title.
A823.4

Typeset in Geist Serifa and The Wall.

Printed in Singapore

10 9 8 7 6 5 4 3 2 1   8 9 / 0 1 2

THE VERY CRANKY BEAR

NICK BLAND

A Scholastic Press book from Scholastic Australia

In the Jingle Jangle Jungle on a cold and rainy day,
four little friends found a perfect place to play.

Moose had marvelous antlers and Lion, a golden mane.
Zebra had fantastic stripes and Sheep . . . well, Sheep was plain.

None of them had noticed that someone else was there.

Sleeping in that cave was a very cranky . . .

BEAR!

"ROAAAAR," went the cranky bear,

"ROAR, ROAR, ROAR!"

He gnashed his teeth and stomped his feet
and chased them out the door.

So in the Jingle Jangle Jungle on a cold and rainy day,
four little friends had nowhere warm to play.

"Wait a minute," said Zebra,
as she scratched her furry chin.
"Maybe if we cheered him up,
he'd let us come back in."

"If I did not have stripes," said Zebra,
"I'd be cranky too.
We should give that bear some stripes,
that's what we should do."

"Stripes are silly," Moose complained,
"especially on a bear.
My antlers always cheer me up,
let's give that bear a pair."

"No, no, no, no, no," said Lion,
"antlers are a bore!
A golden mane like mine," he said,
"would cheer him up for sure."

So Zebra fetched a tin of mud
and Lion, some grass of gold.

Moose got two big branches,
and Sheep . . . well, Sheep got cold.

Sheep was getting worried.
"They've been eaten up for sure!"

And then, from in the cave,
there came a very cranky . . .

"ROAAAAR."

Zebra, Lion and Moose ran out and Bear was right behind them.
They hid behind the bushes where they hoped he wouldn't find them.

"Why is he still cranky, he's got antlers, stripes and mane?
Before we gave him those," Lion said, "he looked so very plain!"

As Bear stormed back inside the cave,
he turned and roared at Sheep.

"ALL I REALLY WANT," he said,

"IS A QUIET PLACE TO SLEEP!"

So she fetched a pair of clippers and she clipped off half her wool.

She stuffed it in a cotton bag until the bag was full.

She tip-toed back inside the cave. "Excuse me, Bear," she said.
"Would you like a pillow for underneath your head?"

"Well, thank you very much," said Bear and soon he fell asleep.
Maybe he was dreaming of a plain, but thoughtful sheep.